I DIDN'T EVEN **KNOW** MY PARENTS. THEY **DIED** WHEN I WAS SMALL. I LIVE WITH MY **UNCLE**, AND HE'S NOT THERE MUCH **EITHER**.

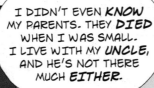

THERE'S NOT MUCH I CAN **SAY** ABOUT MY FAMILY.

I HAVE A SORT OF HOUSEKEEPER INSTEAD, BECAUSE HE'S ALWAYS AWAY ON **BUSINESS**.

CORNWALL

"HE'S GOT A REALLY **BORING** JOB."

"HE'S A **BANK SUPERVISOR**. HE'S IN CHARGE OF **CUSTOMER CARE**."

BOOM!

KER.

DUNK!

"THE THING ABOUT MY UNCLE IS, HE'S NOT VERY EASY TO **PIN DOWN.**"

BRAKKA BRAKKA BRAKKA B

?

SCR EEEECH

!?

VRRRRRM

RI D3R

"I WOULDN'T SAY *I* WAS MUCH LIKE HIM..."

BEETHOVEN
DISC 3 02:56

BEEP

WHIRRRR

KLIK!

0
FRONT MISSILE LAUNCH
REAR MISSILE LAUNCH
EJECTOR SEAT

0

FRONT MISS

TARGET LOCKED

REA MISS

DIT

DIT

DIIIIIIII...

HEY, SABINA.

OH...

HI, ALEX.

I WAS **WONDERING**... DO YOU WANT TO **DO** SOMETHING THIS WEEKEND?

NO.

I MEAN, **I CAN'T.**

I HAVE **RIDING LESSONS** ON SATURDAY, AND THEN I'M GOING **OUT** WITH MY MUM AND DAD.

OH!

SORRY...

IT DOESN'T MATTER.

MAYBE **NEXT** WEEKEND!

WHATEVER.

BEEP BEEP

BANG

BANG BANG

STORMBREAKER

ANTHONY HOROWITZ

Adapted by Antony Johnston

Illustrated by
Kanako Damerum
& Yuzuru Takasaki

WALKER
BOOKS

PATRIOT?

FORASMUCH AS
IT HATH **PLEASED**
ALMIGHTY GOD, OF
HIS GREAT **MERCY**...

WHIRRR...

...TO TAKE **UNTO**
HIMSELF THE SOUL
OF OUR DEAR
BROTHER HERE
DEPARTED...

...WE THEREFORE COMMIT HIS BODY TO THE **GROUND**, IN **SURE AND CERTAIN HOPE** OF THE RESURRECTION TO **ETERNAL LIFE**.

AMEN.

COME ON, LET'S JUST GO **HOME**.

ALEX?

MY NAME IS **JOHN CRAWFORD**.

I'M WITH THE **ROYAL & GENERAL BANK**, AND I WANT YOU TO KNOW YOU HAVE ALL OUR CONDOLENCES.

IT'S AN ABSOLUTE **TRAGEDY**. A **CAR ACCIDENT!** IF ONLY HE'D BEEN WEARING A **SEAT BELT**...

THANK YOU—

THIS IS **ALAN BLUNT**, THE BANK **CHAIRMAN**.

HE'D LIKE A WORD.

DID YOU **MEAN** WHAT YOU **SAID**? ABOUT LOOKING **AFTER** ME?

OF **COURSE** I DID! COME ON, YOU **KNOW** I WOULDN'T LEAVE YOU. ANYWAY, WHO **ELSE** IS THERE?

BUT WILL YOU BE **ALLOWED** TO? I MEAN, WE'RE NOT EVEN **RELATED**.

I'VE BEEN **LIVING** WITH YOU FOR **NINE YEARS**. HOW MUCH **MORE** RELATED DO YOU WANT TO BE?

WAS IT JUST **ME**, OR WAS THERE SOMETHING ABOUT THOSE **BANKERS** THAT STRUCK YOU AS **WEIRD**?

JACK---!

! HEY THAT'S ALL **IAN'S** STUFF! WHAT ARE YOU **DOING**?

HEY!

BRooooo...

SOUTH LONDON

BUT I DIDN'T GET THE *PAPERWORK*...

JUST *DO* IT, HARRY. I'VE GOT TO GO TO *LIVERPOOL STREET*.

THE *STATION*?

WHERE *ELSE*, YOU BERK? I'M TAKING THEM THE *STUFF*...

WOW...

SKREEEEEEE

WHAT—?

?

BRAKKA

BRAKKA

BRAKKA

BRAKKA

HEY—

EURGH!

I COULDN'T BELIEVE WHAT I WAS *DOING*. THIS GUY JUST CAME *AT* ME, AND...

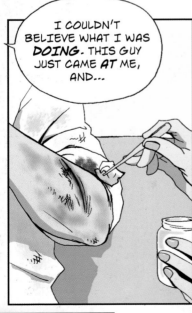

WHAT WERE *THEY*—

—OW!

—*DOING*, JACK? AND WHY WERE THEY *HERE*?

COME *UPSTAIRS* AND SEE FOR *YOURSELF*...

CHELSEA

IAN RIDER
A TRUE PATRIOT

I DON'T *BELIEVE* THIS. I DON'T BELIEVE *ANY* OF IT.

WHERE IS HE *NOW?*

WE CAN'T TELL YOU THAT. I'M *SORRY.*

YOU'RE *SORRY?!* WHAT ARE YOU SORRY *ABOUT?* TAKING HIM OUT OF *SCHOOL?* TRYING TO TURN HIM INTO SOMETHING...

ALEX ISN'T A *SPY!* HE'S *FOURTEEN YEARS OLD!*

THAT'S WHAT MAKES HIM *USEFUL* TO US.

AND WHAT HAPPENS IF HE GETS *HURT?* WHAT IF HE'S *KILLED?* COULD YOU *LIVE* WITH THAT?

I WORKED WITH IAN RIDER FOR NINE YEARS. *NINE YEARS,* AND I NEVER KNEW *ANYTHING* ABOUT THIS.

BUT I'M WARNING YOU, IF ANYTHING *HAPPENS* TO ALEX...

IT *WON'T.* WE'LL LOOK AFTER HIM, I *PROMISE* YOU.

BY THE WAY, HE ASKED ME TO GIVE YOU *THIS.*

IT'S YOUR *VISA.* AND IT'S *PERMANENT.*

HFF

HFF

KEEP THAT GUN ABOVE YOUR HEAD...

GBBL RGBR LRGR GLBR GR GL LBRGR!

BRECON BEACONS

YOU'RE NOT IN THE *PLAYGROUND* NOW, CUB! *MOVE IT!*

LET ME GIVE YOU A *HAND,* CUB.

NO, *WAI...T!*

AAAAAAAAH

BLOOP!

HAHAHA!

HAHAHA HAHA!

HAHAHAHA!

KIYAAA!

KRASH

THERE'S A **FIREPLACE**.

HOW DID **YOU** KNOW?

I SAW THE **CHIMNEY** ON THE WAY IN.

THE KID'S RIGHT. IT'S **CLEAR**.

YOU CAN'T. YOU'RE TOO BIG.

YEAH, **RIGHT**. YOU THINK THEY'D JUST **LEAVE** IT IF THEY THOUGHT WE COULD ALL CLIMB **UP**?

SPLOSH!

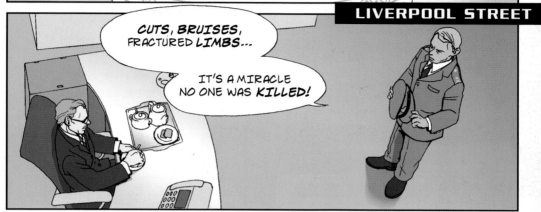

CUTS, BRUISES, FRACTURED *LIMBS*...

IT'S A MIRACLE NO ONE WAS *KILLED!*

HE'S NOT A *CHILD*, HE'S A *LETHAL WEAPON.*

I'M *VERY* SORRY, MAJOR. WE WILL BE *TALKING* TO OUR MAN.

SORRY, *BOY.*

HE'S READY.

AND FINALLY,

THE MOST **GENEROUS** GIFT **EVER MADE** TO THE BRITISH NATION.

HEADLINES: EVERY SCHO~~OL IN~~ THE UK TO BE GI~~VEN~~ THE STORMBR~~EAKER~~

THE **STORMBREAKER** HAS BEEN CALLED THE MOST **SOPHISTICATED** PERSONAL COMPUTER OF THE 21ST CENTURY...

...AND LAST MONTH, ITS MULTIBILLIONAIRE INVENTOR, **DARRIUS SAYLE**, MADE HIS ASTONISHING **ANNOUNCEMENT**.

LIVE

THAT'S **RIGHT**, VIVIEN. I WANT TO GIVE A **FREE STORMBREAKER** TO **EVERY** SCHOOL IN THE COUNTRY.

~~SO~~PHISTICATED PC.

AND WHILE I'M **AT** IT, I WOULDN'T MIND GIVING **YOU** ONE TOO.

LIVE

REALLY, MR SAYLE!

PC.　　DARRIUS SAYLE S~~AYS~~　　~~C~~ONTRIBU~~TES~~

THE **PRIME MINISTER** HAS GIVEN HIS FULL SUPPORT...

THIS IS A **WONDERFUL** OPPORTUNITY FOR BRITISH SCHOOLS, AND I'M **HONOURED** THAT MR SAYLE HAS ASKED **ME** TO PRESS THE BUTTON THAT WILL BRING ALL THE COMPUTERS **ON-LINE**.

~~SCH~~OOL IN THE UK TO BE GIVEN THE STORMBREAKER.

...JUST AS IT HAS **RECENTLY** COME TO LIGHT THAT HE AND MR SAYLE WERE AT **SCHOOL** TOGETHER.

FORTUNE

Inside Darrius Sayle

~~T~~HE EDUCATION SYSTEM.　　THE STORMBREAKER IS TH~~E~~

WE DON'T **TRUST** HIM.

WHY NOT?

WELL, WE DON'T TRUST **ANYONE**. IT'S SORT OF WHAT WE'RE **FOR**.

KLIK

WE ALWAYS **THOUGHT** DARRIUS SAYLE WAS TOO **GOOD** TO BE **TRUE**. SO, SIX MONTHS AGO, WE SENT AN AGENT TO KEEP AN **EYE** ON HIM.

YOU MEAN MY **UNCLE**.

YES.

SAYLE HAS A **MANUFACTURING PLANT** IN **CORNWALL**, BUILT ON TOP OF WHAT USED TO BE A **TIN MINE**. IAN RIDER WENT THERE AS A **SECURITY GUARD**...

...AND HE **FOUND** SOMETHING. IN HIS LAST MESSAGE TO US, HE MENTIONED A **VIRUS**.

A **COMPUTER VIRUS**...?

WE DON'T KNOW. HE WAS ON HIS WAY TO **TELL** US, BUT HE NEVER ARRIVED.

SOMETHING'S GOING ON. WE NEED TO GET SOMEONE **IN** THERE TO TAKE A LOOK **AROUND**,

AND THIS MAY BE OUR **LAST CHANCE**.

DISK DRIVE WORLD

COMPETITION WINNER
Kevin Blake

WHY *ME?*

THIS IS *KEVIN BLAKE,* A COMPUTER NERD. SIX WEEKS AGO HE WON A *COMPETITION* IN THIS MAGAZINE.

EVER *READ* IT?

I'LL SHOW YOU.

...

THE *FIRST PRIZE* WAS A *VISIT* TO CORNWALL AND A CHANCE TO TRY OUT THE *STORMBREAKER.*

HE'S DUE TO ARRIVE *TOMORROW.*

IT'S A *PR STUNT.* I IMAGINE MR SAYLE IS TRYING TO SHOW THE WORLD WHAT A *NICE MAN* HE IS. GET A *KIDDY* IN TO SEE THE WORKS.

YOU'LL TAKE KEVIN'S PLACE.

BUT I'M NOTHING *LIKE* HIM.

DISK DRIVE WORLD

COMPETITION WINNER
Kevin Blake

WE'VE SPOKEN TO THE *EDITOR.*

!!

THERE'S JUST ONE **PROBLEM**...

I DON'T KNOW ANYTHING **ABOUT** COMPUTERS. I'M **NOT** A NERD.

BUT YOU SOON **WILL** BE.

WE ONLY HAVE **THREE DAYS** LEFT. THERE'S A LAUNCH AT THE **SCIENCE MUSEUM** NEXT FRIDAY. **70,000** STORMBREAKER COMPUTERS GOING LIVE...

...

WE **DON'T** WANT YOU TO GET INTO ANY **TROUBLE**, ALEX. JUST TAKE A LOOK **AROUND**. AND BE CAREFUL OF SAYLE. HE MAY **SEEM** CHARMING...

...BUT HE'S ABOUT AS CHARMING AS A **SNAKE**.

JUST KEEP YOUR **EYES** OPEN AND REPORT **BACK**.

BUT HOW WILL I DO **THAT?**

WE'LL SUPPLY YOU WITH A **TELECOMMUNICATIONS DEVICE**. THAT AND...

OTHER GADGETS.

I GET **GADGETS?**

EVENING NEWS

SAYLE LAUNCHES THE STORMBREAKER

IF YOU PAT HIS **HEAD,**

HIS **TAIL** WAGS.

HE ALSO OBEYS CERTAIN **VOICE COMMANDS...**

ROLL OVER!

KLUNK!

DELIGHTFUL, DON'T YOU THINK? WE ALSO HAVE ROBOT **CATS** AND **RODENTS—**

EXCUSE ME.

I'M LOOKING FOR SOMETHING TO TAKE TO **CORNWALL.**

GEEE

GEEEE

AH.

CORNWALL, YES.

COME WITH ME...

GEE GEEE

FOUNTAIN PEN.

NOT USED BY MANY YOUNG PEOPLE THESE DAYS, ALAS...

A MODIFIED NINTENDO DS. WHAT IT DOES DEPENDS ON THE CARTRIDGE THAT YOU PLACE IN IT.

THE NIB CAN BE FIRED FROM A RANGE OF SIX METRES, AND THE INK IS SODIUM PENTATHOL. WHOEVER YOU HIT WILL DO EXACTLY WHAT YOU TELL THEM FOR THE NEXT SIX HOURS.

BUT I'VE SAVED THE BEST 'TIL LAST...

SLIP IN THIS GAME, CALLUP, AND IT'S A PDA SCANNER AND TRANSMITTER. THAT'S HOW YOU KEEP IN TOUCH WITH US.

PANIC STATION IS A BUG-FINDER AND SONIC INTENSIFIER. YOU CAN HEAR A CONVERSATION TWO ROOMS AWAY.

THIS ONE IS CALLED GREEN SCREEN. IT TURNS THE WHOLE THING INTO A SMOKE BOMB, WITH A FIVE SECOND FUSE.

WHAT ABOUT MARIO KART?

OH, THAT'S JUST A GAME.

I THOUGHT YOU MIGHT LIKE IT FOR THE FLIGHT.

GREETINGS FROM CORNWALL

IT'S FROM **CORNWALL!**

BUT HE DIDN'T MEAN YOU TO GO THERE **NOW,** ALEX. THAT'S NOT WHAT HE **MEANT...**

IT'S ONLY A FEW DAYS, JACK.

I'LL BE **CAREFUL.**

YOU REALLY **PROMISE** ME?

I PROMISE.

AND ALEX...

WHAT?

ANOTHER **GADGET?**

WHAT IS IT, A **LOCKPICK?** DOES IT **EXPLODE?**

NO, ALEX.

IT **CLEANS** YOUR **TEETH.**

KEVIN BLAKE!

MRS VOLE, IS THAT RIGHT? I'M THE EDITOR OF *DISC DRIVE WORLD*...

THEN THIS MUST BE *KEVIN*, JA?

THAT'S ME.

GUT. YOU SHOULD SAY *GOODBYE* NOW.

GOODBYE, KEVIN! I HOPE YOU FIND YOUR STAY VERY *INFORMATIVE!*

←ARRIVAL

CAR PARK→

I'M SURE IT *WILL* BE...

I AM *NADIA VOLE.* I WORK FOR *MR SAYLE* IN *PR.*

PUBLIC RELATIONS?

JA. THIS IS *PORT TALLON.* A *FISHING VILLAGE.*

PORT TALLON
Welcome
Careful Drivers

NICE PLACE.

NOT IF YOU ARE A *FISH.*

IT'S **NINETY-NINE PER CENT WATER**. IT HAS NO **BRAINS**, AND NO **ANUS**.

THE **MAN OF WAR** IS AN **OUTSIDER**.

IT'S **SILENT**, YET IT DEMANDS **RESPECT**. THOSE **TENTACLES** ARE COVERED IN **NEMATOCYSTS**... STINGING CELLS. IF YOU CAME INTO **CONTACT** WITH THEM, YOU'D DIE A VERY **MEMORABLE** DEATH.

... I THINK I'M GOING TO **LIKE** YOU.

I'M TOO **YOUNG** TO DIE.

NO, NO, **NO**. I WOULDN'T BELIEVE **THAT**.

YOU'RE **NEVER** TOO YOUNG TO DIE.

WHAT THE...?

HIYA, CUDDLES.

MR SAYLE, THE **AMERICAN AMBASSADOR** IS ON LINE ONE.

FZZZZZzzzz

IT SEEMS I'M **NOT** GOING TO BE ABLE TO **JOIN** YOU FOR LUNCH AFTER **ALL**, BUT I HOPE YOU'LL HAVE **DINNER** WITH ME TONIGHT.

IT'S BEEN QUITE A **WHILE** SINCE I FOUND MYSELF FACE TO FACE WITH A BRITISH **SCHOOL KID**... I CAN'T **WAIT** TO HEAR WHAT YOU THINK OF THE **STORMBREAKER**.

THIS IS MY PERSONAL ASSISTANT, **MR GRIN**.

HE SEEMS TO HAVE **CUT** HIMSELF **SHAVING**.

MR GRIN USED TO WORK IN A **CIRCUS**. IT WAS A NOVELTY **KNIFE-THROWING** ACT. FOR A **CLIMAX**, HE CAUGHT A **SPINNING KNIFE** BETWEEN HIS **TEETH**...

MURGH.

...UNTIL **ONE** NIGHT, HIS MOTHER **WAVED** TO HIM FROM THE FRONT ROW AND HE MADE A **MISTAKE** WITH HIS **TIMING**.

HE CAN'T **TALK**, BUT HE'LL SHOW YOU TO YOUR **ROOM** AND WE'LL MEET AGAIN **TONIGHT**. OKAY?

HAVE **FUN**.

BEEP

HMMM.

TIK!

SKEHTECH

YAAAAAA!

KNOCK KNOCK

IT IS *TIME* FOR YOU TO SEE THE *STORMBREAKER.*

YOU ARE THE *FIRST* CHILD TO EXPERIENCE THE *POWER*, THE *WORLD DOMINATION* OF THE STORMBREAKER.

THIS MODEL HAS BEEN ALREADY LOADED WITH *HIGHLY DEVELOPED* PROGRAMS FOR ALL ASPECTS OF THE *SCHOOL CURRICULUM.*

SO, UM... WHERE *IS* IT?

YOU ARE *STANDING* IN IT. IT IS THE *STORMBREAKER PROTOTYPE.*

STEP ONTO THE *PLATFORM.*

DOES IT HAVE *PINBALL?*

BE *STILL,* PLEASE, WHILE WE *SCAN* YOU.

JA! WHO **TAUGHT** YOU ABOUT COMPUTERS, KEVIN?

MY UNCLE.

HE IS A COMPUTER **WHIZ-KING**?

NO, HE WAS A **SECURITY GUARD**. BUT HE **DIED**.

YOU'RE USING **SLICE-MATRIX VIRTUAL REALITY** SOFTWARE, AREN'T YOU?

HOW DID THAT **HAPPEN**?

I DON'T **KNOW**.

BUT **ONE** DAY I'LL FIND **OUT**.

PROGRAMMING COMPLETE

MAYBE. BUT **NOT** TODAY.

YOU WILL START WITH **SCIENCE**. PRESS **ENTER** TO BEGIN.

SCIENCE, EH? GREAT...

...NOT.

UH-OH.

GOOD **MORNING**, MR SAYLE.

IS IT **READY** FOR ME?

YES, SIR. THIS WAY, PLEASE...

!

...THE **BACK-UP** SYSTEM.

IT WILL SEND OUT A **SIGNAL** THAT WILL **INSTANTLY** ACTIVATE ALL **SEVENTY THOUSAND** COMPUTERS.

OF COURSE, IT SHOULDN'T BE **NEEDED**.

NO.

IT'S **EXCELLENT**. VERY—

—GOOD.

HMMM.

KEVIN?

DIESER **VERDAMMTE** JUNGE...

HMMM.

NICE **WEATHER** FOR THE TIME OF YEAR.

...BUT *ANYWAY*.

TELL ME, HOW DID YOU LIKE THE *STORMBREAKER?*

IT'S COOL.

"COOL." IS THAT *ALL* YOU CAN *SAY?*

YOU KNOW, KEVIN, IT STRIKES ME THAT YOU DON'T *TALK* VERY MUCH LIKE A COMPUTER *ENTHUSIAST*. NOR DO YOU *LOOK* LIKE ONE.

I'D HAVE SAID THE SAME ABOUT *YOU*, MR SAYLE.

GOOD **POINT**.

I'VE VERY MUCH **ENJOYED** MEETING YOU, KEVIN. I'M SURE YOU'LL HAVE A **LOT** TO TALK ABOUT WHEN YOU GET BACK TO **SCHOOL**.

SURE.

AND WHEN WE **LAUNCH** THE STORMBREAKERS TOMORROW...

I'LL BE THINKING **PARTICULARLY** OF YOU.

BRRRRING

CHELSEA

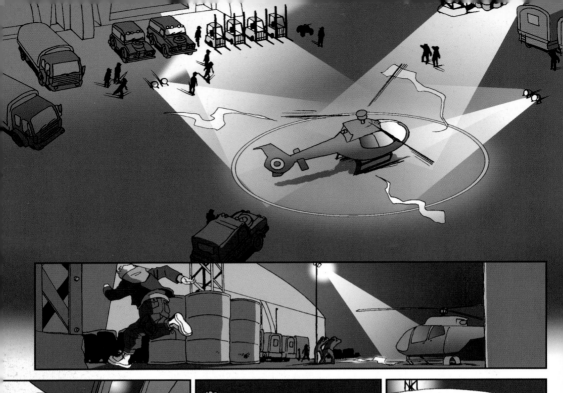

MR GREGOROVICH!

LET US **START**.

R-5

I'M GLAD YOU WERE ABLE TO **JOIN** US TONIGHT.

I DIDN'T **REALIZE** YOU WERE GOING TO COME **PERSONALLY**.

I'M **SO** SORRY.

I WON'T DO THAT AGAIN.

NO.

YOU WILL **NOT**.

BLAM!

MY PEOPLE DO NOT LIKE **MISTAKES**.

GET **BACK** TO **WORK!**

I TOLD YOU I **DIDN'T** WANT TO BE **INTERRUPTED**...

...UNLESS IT WAS **IMPORTANT**.

AND **IS** IT?

LONDON

WE JUST GOT **THIS** FROM ALEX RIDER.

"GREGOROVICH"? **YASSEN** GREGOROVICH?

IT **HAS** TO BE.

I THOUGHT HE WAS STILL IN **NORTH KOREA**.

IT SEEMS **NOT**.

THIS IS THE **PROOF** YOU NEED, ALAN. THE STORMBREAKER **LAUNCH** IS LESS THAN **24 HOURS** AWAY. **CANCEL** IT.

YES. YOU'RE **RIGHT**.

I'LL PUT A **CALL** INTO **DOWNING STREET**.

AND GET ALEX **OUT**.

HE'LL BE **FLYING** OUT AT TWELVE O'CLOCK TOMORROW **ANYWAY**. NO POINT MAKING SAYLE — OR **GREGOROVICH**, COME TO THAT — **SUSPICIOUS**.

YOU CAN **MEET** HIM IF YOU LIKE. TAKE HIM OUT FOR AN **ICE CREAM**.

WHAT?

HE'S DONE VERY **WELL**. HE DESERVES A **TREAT**.

SNAP.

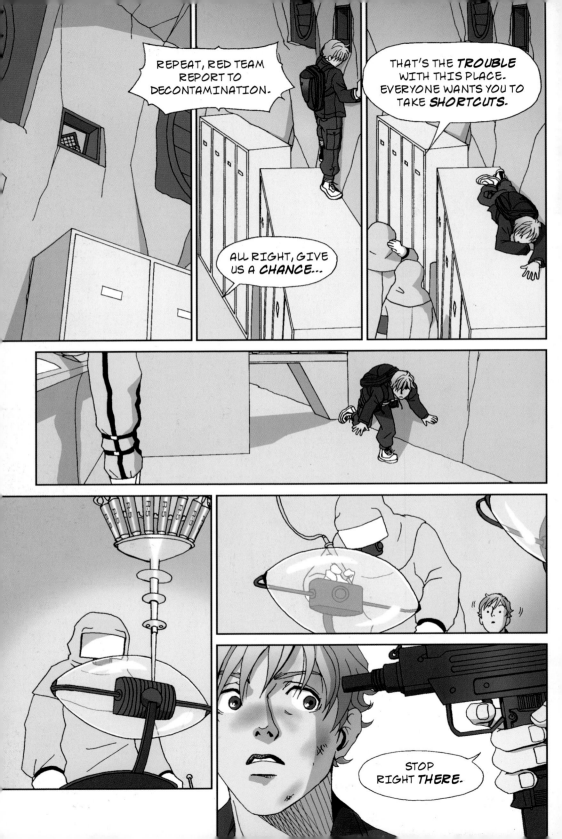

UP THERE.

THANKS.

CATCH!

!

BRAKKA

SPTANG

BRAKKA

BRAKKA

STOP!
STOP!

SPTANG

YOU *IDIOT!* YOU MUST NOT FIRE **BULLETS** IN HERE!

OH!

OF COURSE, I'M **SORRY**. I WON'T DO THAT...

...AGAIN?

NO. YOU WILL **NOT**.

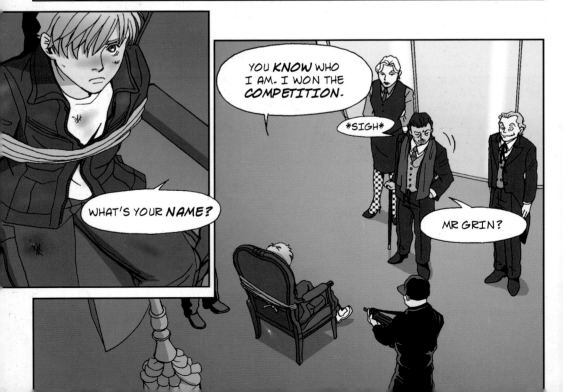

THUNK

IF **THIS** IS HOW YOU TREAT THE **WINNER**, I'D **HATE** TO SEE WHAT HAPPENED TO THE **RUNNER-UP**.

YOU'RE **NOT** KEVIN BLAKE.

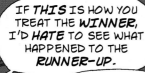

YOU'RE **ALEX RIDER**.

YOUR **UNCLE** WAS PRETENDING TO BE A **SECURITY** GUARD, BUT **YASSEN GREGOROVICH** DEALT WITH **HIM...**

...AND **MIG** SENT **YOU** TO TAKE HIS PLACE.

SENDING A **FOURTEEN-YEAR-OLD** TO DO THEIR **DIRTY WORK**. NOT VERY **BRITISH**, I'D HAVE SAID. NOT **CRICKET**.

WHAT ARE YOU **DOING** HERE? WE **KNOW** YOU'RE PUTTING SOME KIND OF **VIRUS** INTO THE STORMBREAKER...

OH! IT'S... IT'S NOT A **COMPUTER** VIRUS, IS IT?

IT'S **THE REAL THING!**

VERY **CLEVER**, ALEX.

IT'S CALLED **R5**... A **GENETICALLY MODIFIED** VIRUS.

IT'S **VERY** NASTY.

BUT YOU'LL KILL **THOUSANDS** OF PEOPLE!

WHAT?

NO, NO, DON'T BE **SILLY**.

I'LL KILL **MILLIONS** OF THEM.

ALL BECAUSE YOU WERE **BULLIED** AT **SCHOOL**?

LOTS OF PEOPLE ARE BULLIED AT SCHOOL, BUT IT DOESN'T TURN **THEM** INTO **RAVING PSYCHOPATHS!**

TIME TO SAY **GOODBYE**, ALEX.

AS YOU MAY HAVE SEEN, I'M **PACKING UP** AND **LEAVING**. I'D **LOVE** TO STAY, BUT I HAVE A RATHER IMPORTANT APPOINTMENT IN **LONDON**.

THUNK

SO I'LL LEAVE YOU TO **NADIA**.

THAT WAS... A GOOD **SHOT**.

EURGH.

ACTUALLY, IT WAS A **NEAR MISS**. YOU SHOULD WATCH YOUR **MOUTH**.

THE JELLYFISH CANNOT **ATTACK** YOU, ALEX. IT HAS, AS YOU **SAID**, NO **BRAINS.**

SPLOSH

SSSSSSS...

HAH

HAH...

BUT YOU WILL **TIRE** SOON. YOU WILL **DRIFT** INTO ITS EMBRACE. AND THEN...

HAH...

...

GLUUUB!

WHAT ARE YOU **DOING,** DU **VERDAMMTES KIND...?!**

?!

KRACK

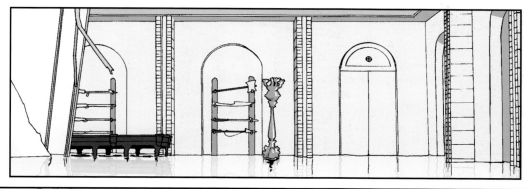

...FINAL DEPARTURE IN TWO MINUTES.

EVACUATE ALL PERSONNEL. REPEAT...

HE'S *ESCAPED!*

OPEN FIRE!

BRAKKA

BRAKKA

BRAKKA

...DEPARTURE IN ONE MINUTE AND THIRTY SECONDS. EVACUATE ALL...

SPTANG

SPTANG

SPTANG

VRRRRRM!

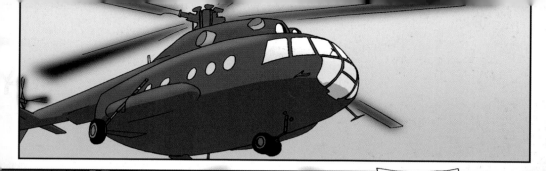

...FINAL DEPARTURE IS NOW. ALL PERSONNEL EVACUATE IMMEDIATELY.

REPEAT, FINAL DEPARTURE...

IMPRESSIVE.

EUUGH!

NUUUH...

ALL RIGHT, MR GRIN.

I WANT YOU TO FLY ME TO *LONDON*. AS *FAST* AS YOU CAN.

YARGH...

HYDE PARK, LONDON

WE DON'T KNOW.

WHAT DO YOU *MEAN*, YOU *DON'T KNOW?* YOU *PROMISED* ME YOU'D LOOK AFTER HIM!

WE DON'T HAVE *TIME* FOR THIS NOW, MISS STARBRIGHT.

THE *PRIME MINISTER* IS...

CLAP

CLAP

CLAP

CLAP

LADIES AND GENTLEMEN, *THANK YOU.*

THE MESSAGE TODAY IS QUITE *CLEAR.*

"AND THAT MESSAGE IS *EDUCATION.* EDUCATION, EDUCATION, AND..."

AND...

UM...

...AND EDUCATION!

AND **THAT** IS WHY I AM **DELIGHTED** TO ACCEPT THE **GENEROUS** OFFER MADE BY ONE OF OUR **FOREMOST ENTREPRENEURS**, AND **MY** OLD SCHOOL COLLEAGUE...

DARRIUS SMELL.

SAYLE!

DARRIUS **SAYLE!**

I WANT YOU TO KEEP FLYING **NORTH** UNTIL YOU RUN OUT OF **FUEL**. THEN YOU CAN **LAND**, OK?

NORGH.

BROOKLAND SCHOOL

YOU CAN LEAVE HIM TO *US*. DON'T *WORRY* ABOUT HIM.

YOU'VE DONE VERY *WELL*, ALEX. BUT YOU SHOULD *GO*, NOW.

WHAT ABOUT *SAYLE?*

...FINE.

HOW COULD THEY LET HIM SLIP *AWAY?*

IT'S NOT YOUR *PROBLEM*. I CAN'T BELIEVE I *EVER* LET YOU GET *MIXED UP* IN ALL THIS.

BUT IT'S *OVER* NOW, AND IT'S TIME YOU CAME *HOME*.

YEAH, BUT WHERE'S HE *GOING*...?

SOMEWHERE *REMOTE* AND *FAR AWAY* WHERE NOBODY WILL *EVER* FIND HIM. LIKE... PARAGUAY.

OR *IOWA*.

JACK! STOP THE *CAR!*

THAT'S IT!

SAYLE TOWER!

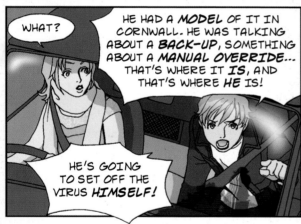

WHAT?

HE HAD A *MODEL* OF IT IN CORNWALL. HE WAS TALKING ABOUT A *BACK-UP*, SOMETHING ABOUT A *MANUAL OVERRIDE...* THAT'S WHERE IT *IS*, AND THAT'S WHERE *HE* IS!

HE'S GOING TO SET OFF THE VIRUS *HIMSELF*!

COME *ON*, PUT YOUR *FOOT* DOWN!

I *CAN'T*!

WHY *NOT?* JACK, HE'LL KILL *EVERYONE*!

BECAUSE, ALEX, YOU'RE NOT IN *CORNWALL* ANY MORE.

WELCOME TO *LONDON TRAFFIC.*

NO...

THANKS, SABINA!

WAIT---!

STOP RIGHT THERE!

NOT *AGAIN*...

WHUD!

!

OOOWOOARRRRRR

SCHOOLBOY TRICK.

BROOKLAND SCHOOL

ALEX!

SABINA! DON'T **DO** THAT!

NOT **HERE**, ANYWAY...

THEY MADE ME SIGN THE **OFFICIAL SECRETS ACT**. I'M NOT ALLOWED TO TELL **ANYONE** WHAT HAPPENED.

ME TOO.

ARE YOU **REALLY** A SPY?

NO.

THAT'S **NOT** WHAT THEY TOLD **ME**...

I'M **NOT**. AND IT **WON'T** HAPPEN **AGAIN**.

NO, OF **COURSE** NOT.

First published 2006 by Walker Books Ltd
87 Vauxhall Walk, London SE11 5HJ

10 9 8 7 6 5 4 3 2 1

This book has been typeset in Lint McCree
and Serpentine Bold
Printed in Italy

British Library Cataloguing in Publication Data:
a catalogue record for this book is available from
the British Library

ISBN-13: 978-1-84428-111-4
ISBN-10: 1-84428-111-6

www.walkerbooks.co.uk

⊕ **ANTHONY HOROWITZ,**
who scripted the movie blockbuster
STORMBREAKER from his own
novel, is one of the most popular
and prolific children's writers
working today. His hugely
successful Alex Rider series
has won numerous awards and
sold over eight million copies
worldwide. He has won the
Red House Children's Book
Award on two occasions, in
2003 for SKELETON KEY and
in 2006 for ARK ANGEL. He also
writes extensively for TV, with
programmes including MIDSOMER
MURDERS, POIROT and FOYLE'S
WAR. He is married to television
producer Jill Green and lives in
north London with his two sons,
Nicholas and Cassian, and their
dog, Lucky.

www.anthonyhorowitz.com

⊕ **ANTONY JOHNSTON,** who
wrote the script for this book,
is the author of nine graphic
novels, including THE LONG
HAUL, JULIUS, THREE DAYS
IN EUROPE and ROSEMARY'S
BACKPACK, and the ongoing
series WASTELAND. He has also
adapted many prose works by Alan
Moore into comics form, and is the
only other writer to have penned
a story for Greg Rucka's award-
winning QUEEN & COUNTRY
series. Antony lives in north-west
England with the three loves of
his life; his partner Marcia, his
dog Connor, and his iMac.

www.mostlyblack.com

⊕ The artwork in this graphic
novel is the work of two artists,
KANAKO DAMERUM and
YUZURU TAKASAKI, who
collaborate on every illustration.
Although living on opposite
sides of the globe, these Japanese
sisters work seamlessly together
via the Internet.

Living and working in Tokyo,
YUZURU produced all the line
work for these illustrations using
traditional means. The quality of
her draughtsmanship comes from
years of honing her skills in the
highly competitive world of manga.

KANAKO lives and works out of
her studio in London. She managed
and directed the project as well
as colouring and rendering the
artwork digitally using her wealth
of knowledge in graphic design.

www.manga-media.com
www.thorogood.net

Collect all 6 Alex Rider books

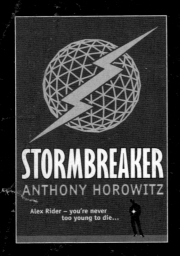

STORMBREAKER
ANTHONY HOROWITZ

Alex Rider – you're never too young to die...

1-84428-092-6

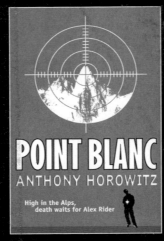

POINT BLANC
ANTHONY HOROWITZ

High in the Alps, death waits for Alex Rider

1-84428-093-4

SKELETON KEY
ANTHONY HOROWITZ

Alex Rider's in deep water – again

1-84428-094-2

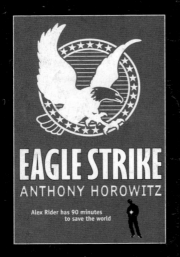

EAGLE STRIKE
ANTHONY HOROWITZ

Alex Rider has 90 minutes to save the world

1-84428-095-0

SCORPIA
ANTHONY HOROWITZ

Once stung, twice as deadly. Alex Rider wants revenge.

0-7445-7051-4

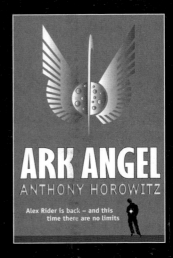

ARK ANGEL
ANTHONY HOROWITZ

Alex Rider is back – and this time there are no limits

0-7445-8324-1

Also available on CD, read by Oliver Chris

Check out www.alexrider.com!